Welcome to
Little Funnies

Little Funnies is a delightful collection of picture books made to put a giggle into storytime.

There are funny stories about a laughing lobster, a daring mouse, a teeny tiny woman, and lots more colourful characters!

Perfect for sharing, these rib-tickling tales will have your little ones coming back for more!

D0320307

TEE HEE!

HA HA!

For my friend Norma,
who loves flowers
P. R.

For my great-niece
Molly, with love
H. C.

First published 2000 by Walker Books Ltd
87 Vauxhall Walk, London SE11 5HJ

This edition published 2007

10 9 8 7 6 5 4 3 2 1

Text © 2000 Phyllis Root
Illustrations © 2000 Helen Craig

The moral rights of the
author/illustrator have been asserted.

This book has been typeset in
Calligraphic Antique.

Printed in China

All rights reserved

British Library Cataloguing in
Publication Data:
a catalogue record for this book is
available from the British Library.

ISBN 978-1-4063-0786-3

www.walkerbooks.co.uk

FOGGY FRIDAY

Written by
Phyllis Root

Illustrated by
Helen Craig

WALKER BOOKS
AND SUBSIDIARIES
LONDON · BOSTON · SYDNEY · AUCKLAND

One foggy Friday morning on
Bonnie Bumble's farm, the rooster
lost his cock-a-doodle-doo.
He tried to crow, but
nothing came out.

So no one could
get up. Even the
flowers stayed
in their beds.

The other animals tried to crow
instead. The pig went,

Even the chicks went,

CHEEP-A-CHOODLE-CHOO!

But nothing worked.
No one got up.

"Something has to be done,"
said Bonnie Bumble.

So she took her bed and went outside to find the rooster's voice.

She peered in the pigpen.

She climbed into the cowshed.

When the fog finally lifted, Bonnie Bumble found the rooster's voice right where he had dropped it.

The rooster was so glad to get his cock-a-doodle-doo, he crowed and crowed. Even the flowers got out of their beds.

COCK-

A-DOODLE-DOO!

Soon everyone was up on Bonnie Bumble's farm.

Everyone but Bonnie.

Bonnie Bumble,
all worn out, went,